Special Effects

Bringing Movies to Life

Nicolas Brasch

Contents

Unimaginable Worlds

Some people enjoy going to the movies to see their favourite actors. Others like dramatic movies or comedies or scary movies. But many people go to the movies because of the special effects. Special effects are the visual illusions, or tricks, that appear in movies, and the methods and techniques film-makers use to create them.

Special effects have been part of movie-making for a long time. The special effects used in movies today are very advanced. They can involve the creation of worlds that are almost unimaginable. Special effects can also make characters do things that actors would not be able to do without **artificial** help. Some special effects are made using computers and software. But they can also be created using machinery and **props** on a film set.

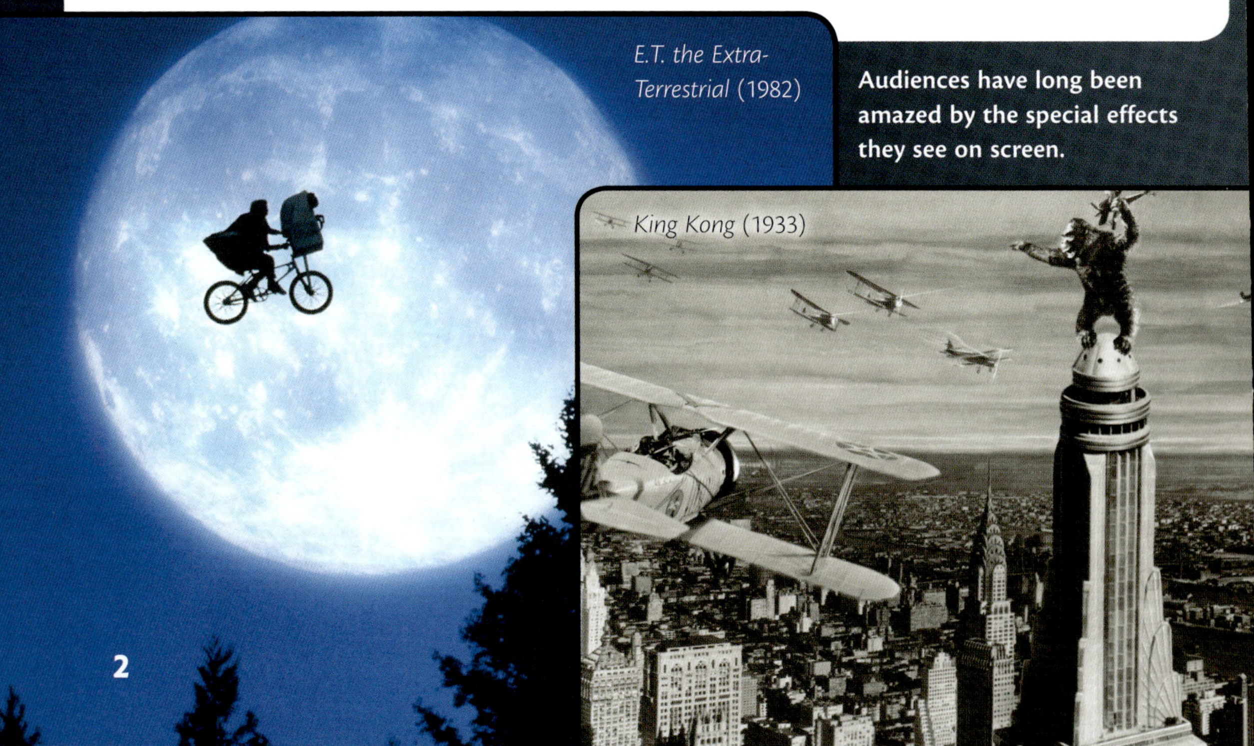

E.T. the Extra-Terrestrial (1982)

King Kong (1933)

Audiences have long been amazed by the special effects they see on screen.

Some special effects can make a movie less expensive to produce. For example, if a scene needs to be shot in the rain, hiring a rain machine is cheaper and easier than moving the entire cast and crew to a place where rain is expected or, alternatively, waiting around a film location until it starts raining. However, some special effects can make up more than half of the total cost of producing a movie – so they need to be well done.

Think and Talk About ...

Special effects are carried out on the set, during filming. Visual effects are carried out after filming is complete, often on a computer, in a phase called "post-production".

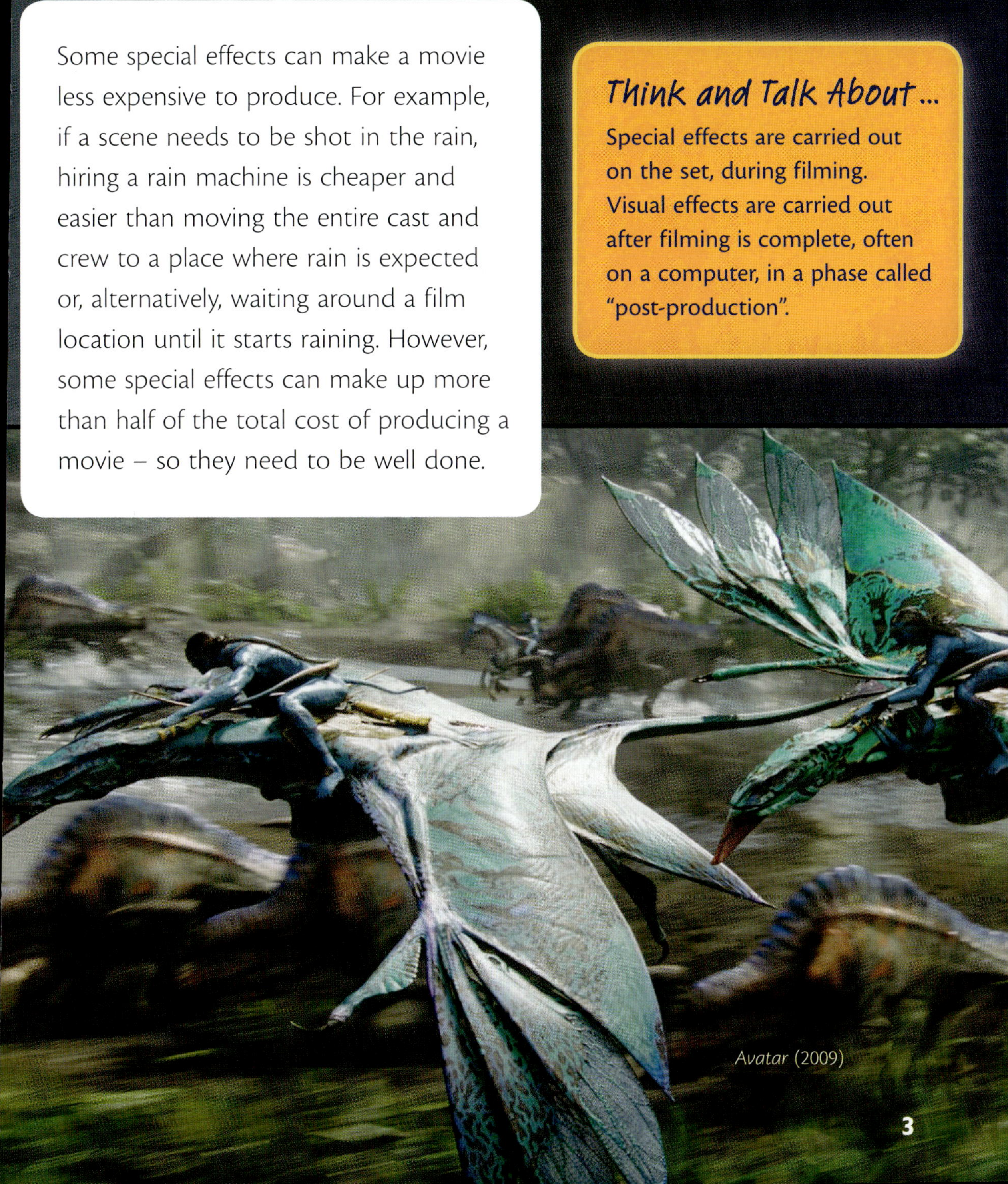

Avatar (2009)

The Stop Trick

The very first special effect used in a movie was called the "stop trick". The stop trick involved stopping the camera in the middle of a scene, rearranging the actors or props, then restarting the camera. When the scene was viewed later by an audience, something would appear to change, as if by magic. For example, an object in a scene might disappear suddenly.

Today, the stop trick would be considered a simple editing task – one that could be done after filming, on a computer, or even a smartphone, with very simple software. But, back in the earliest days of movie-making, special effects were all done on the film set.

French **director** and special-effects **pioneer** Georges Méliès (say: *mel-yez*) discovered the stop trick for himself by accident while filming a street scene in Paris in 1896. His camera became jammed and stopped filming, but the scene continued. When his camera started working again, it resumed filming. When Méliès watched the film, he realised that stopping and restarting a camera deliberately could create some interesting effects within a scene.

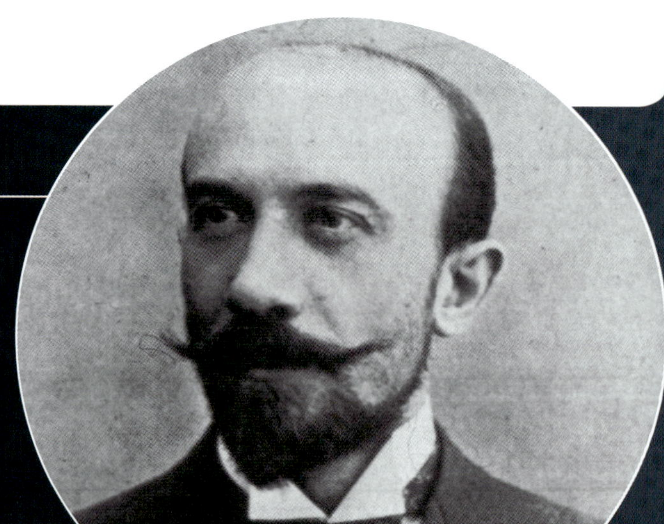

special-effects pioneer Georges Méliès in 1890

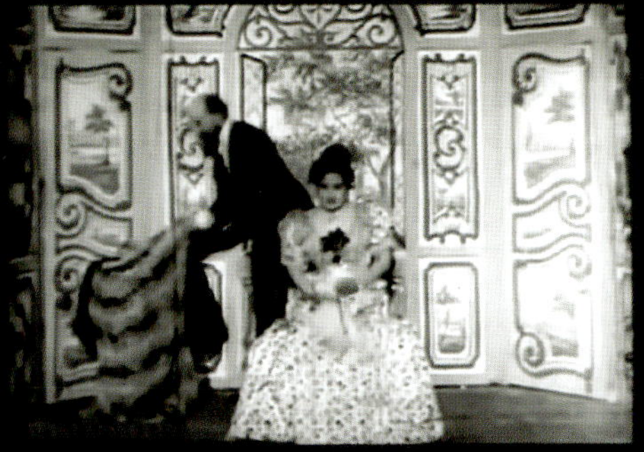

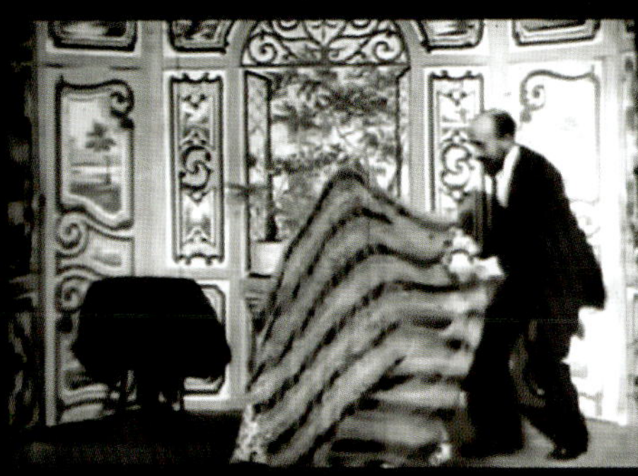

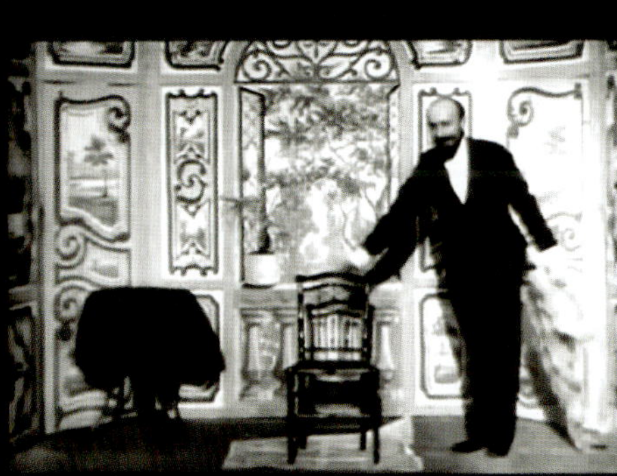

George Méliès used the stop trick to make an actress "disappear" in his movie *The Vanishing Lady* (1896).

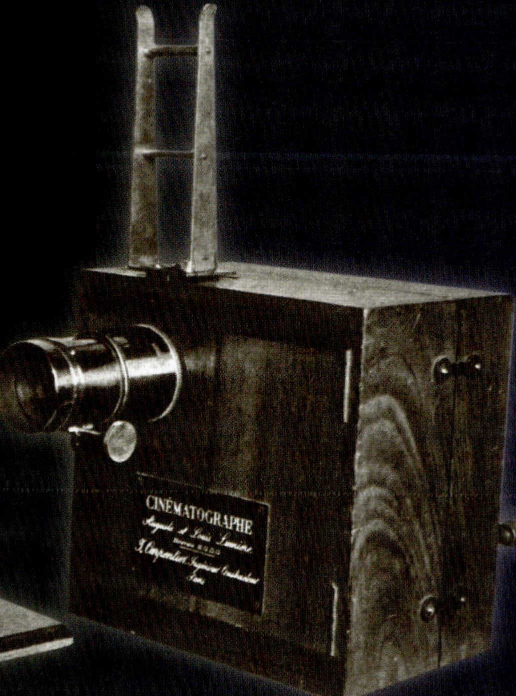

Think and Talk About ...

In 1895, the Lumiere brothers from France invented a device called the *cinématographe.* It consisted of a camera, a printer and a projector.

Fake Blood

Audiences have long been thrilled and terrified by movies with blood. The techniques for showing blood on screen are different, depending on whether the movie is shot in black and white, or in colour.

Before the introduction of colour to films, film-makers could not rely on the colour red to create the effect of blood, so it was important that the consistency, or thickness, of the fake blood looked realistic. The famous twentieth-century film director Alfred Hitchcock tried several substances before deciding that chocolate sauce resembled blood better than anything else. Chocolate sauce is still used to mimic blood in black-and-white movies today.

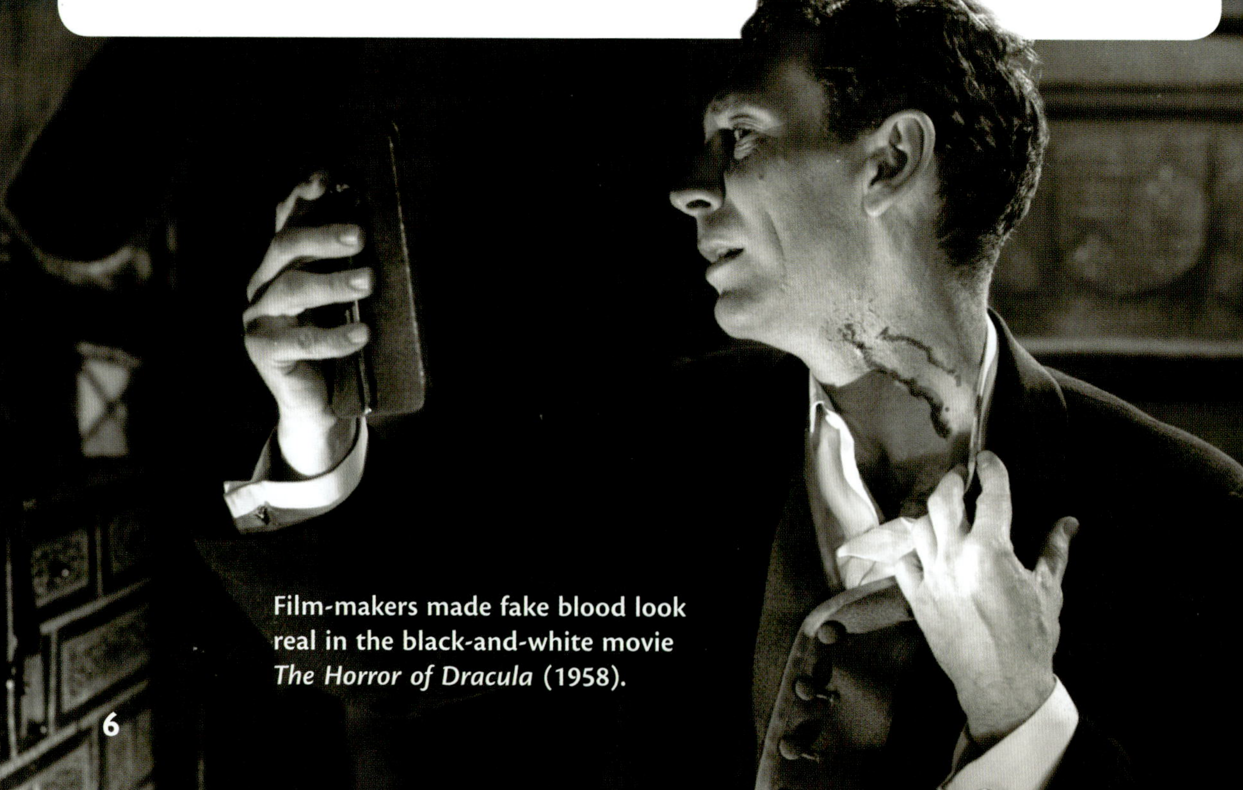

Film-makers made fake blood look real in the black-and-white movie *The Horror of Dracula* (1958).

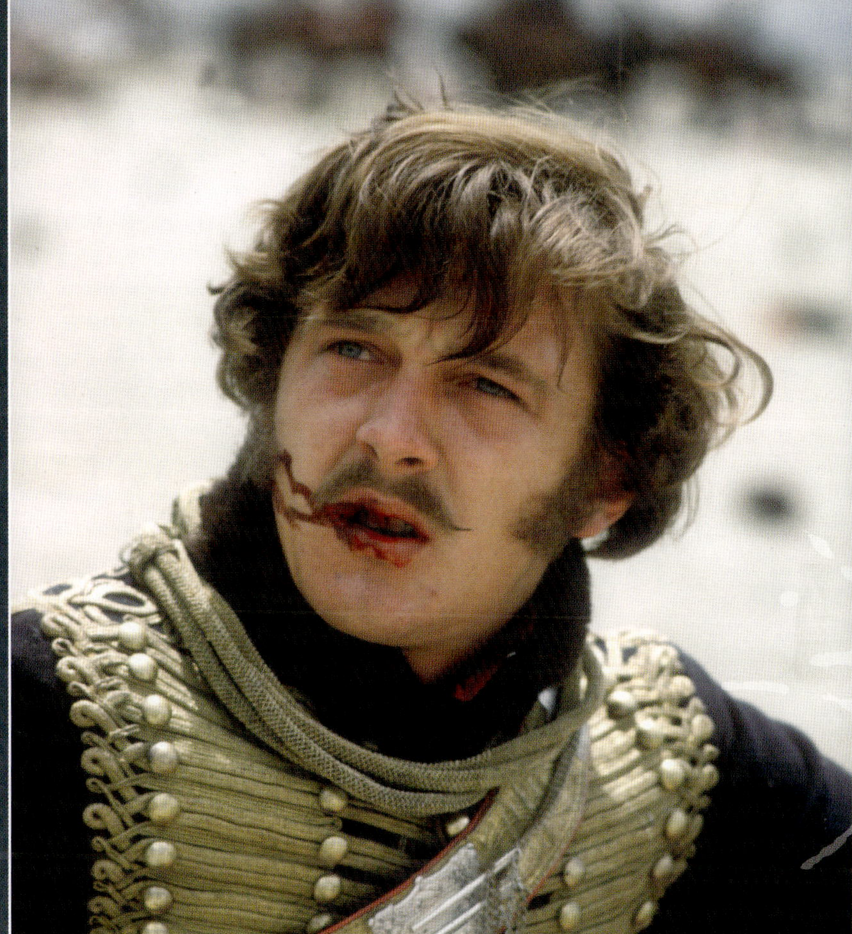

Ingredients in fake blood need to be safe enough for an actor to put in his or her mouth.

The introduction of colour to films brought new challenges for special-effects teams when creating fake blood. Often, fake blood that looked realistic in a laboratory was too bright when filmed under movie lights.

Film-makers discovered that realistic-looking fake blood could be made using ingredients that were poisonous. However, poison could not be used if the blood was to be seen coming from an actor's mouth. As a result, peanut butter became a common ingredient. Peanut butter helped to give the fake blood a realistic colour when mixed with other ingredients. So it was not only safe, but it tasted good, too!

Make Your Own Fake Blood

Goal

To make fake blood to use in your own movies

Materials

You will need:

- a measuring cup
- a bowl
- $\frac{1}{3}$ of a cup of golden syrup
- a teaspoon
- a mixing spoon
- 1 heaped teaspoon of cornflour
- 1 teaspoon of red food dye
- a bottle of chocolate sauce.

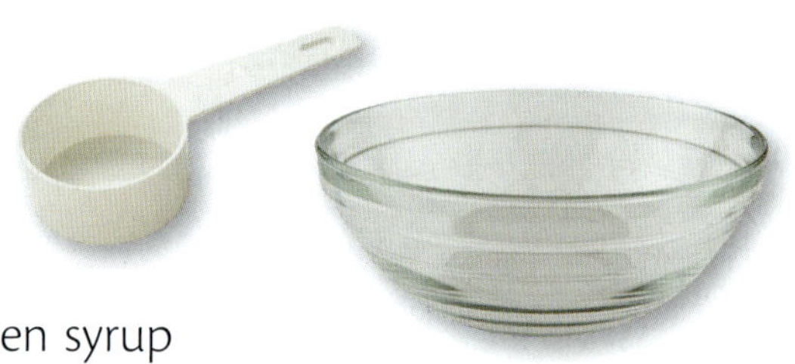

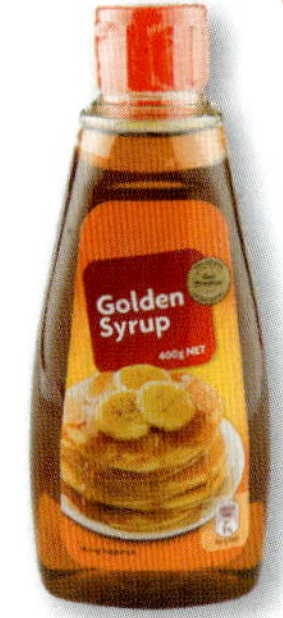

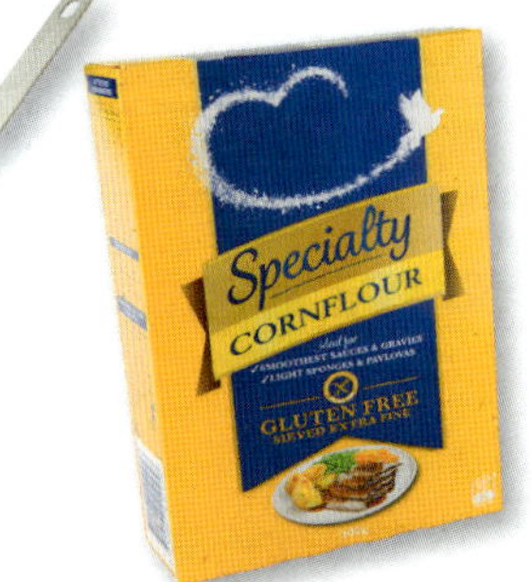

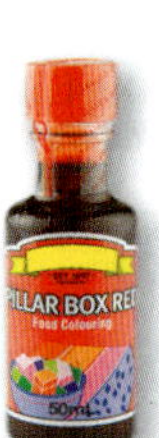

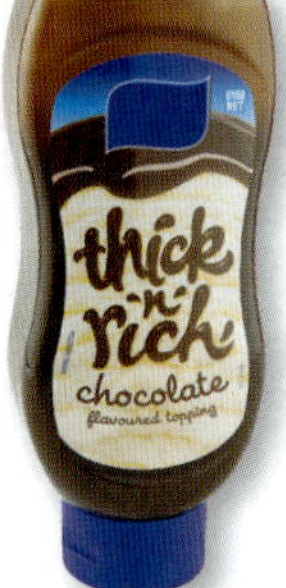

Steps

1. Pour the golden syrup into a bowl.

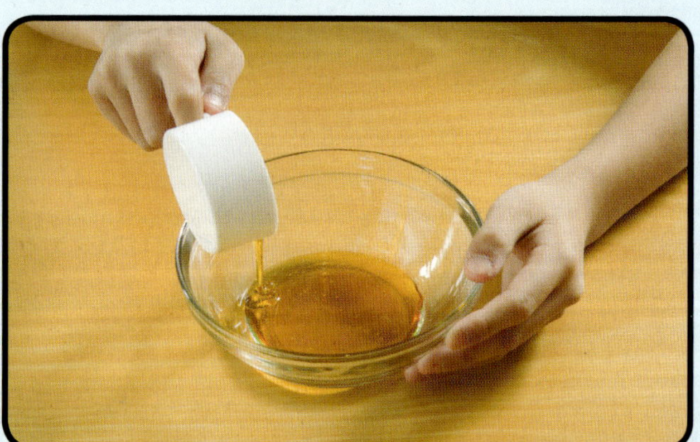

2. Add the heaped teaspoon of cornflour. Mix thoroughly until combined.
3. Add the red food dye. Mix until the dye is evenly combined.
4. Gradually add a few teaspoons of chocolate sauce until the colour of the mixture looks like the colour of blood.
5. Add a pinch more cornflour to thicken the mixture, if required.

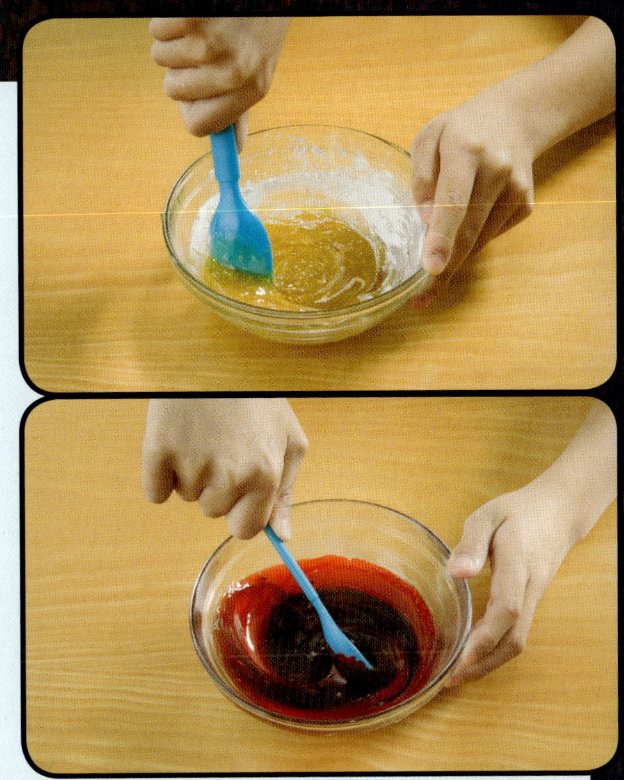

6. Use your fake blood to impress – or scare – your audience!

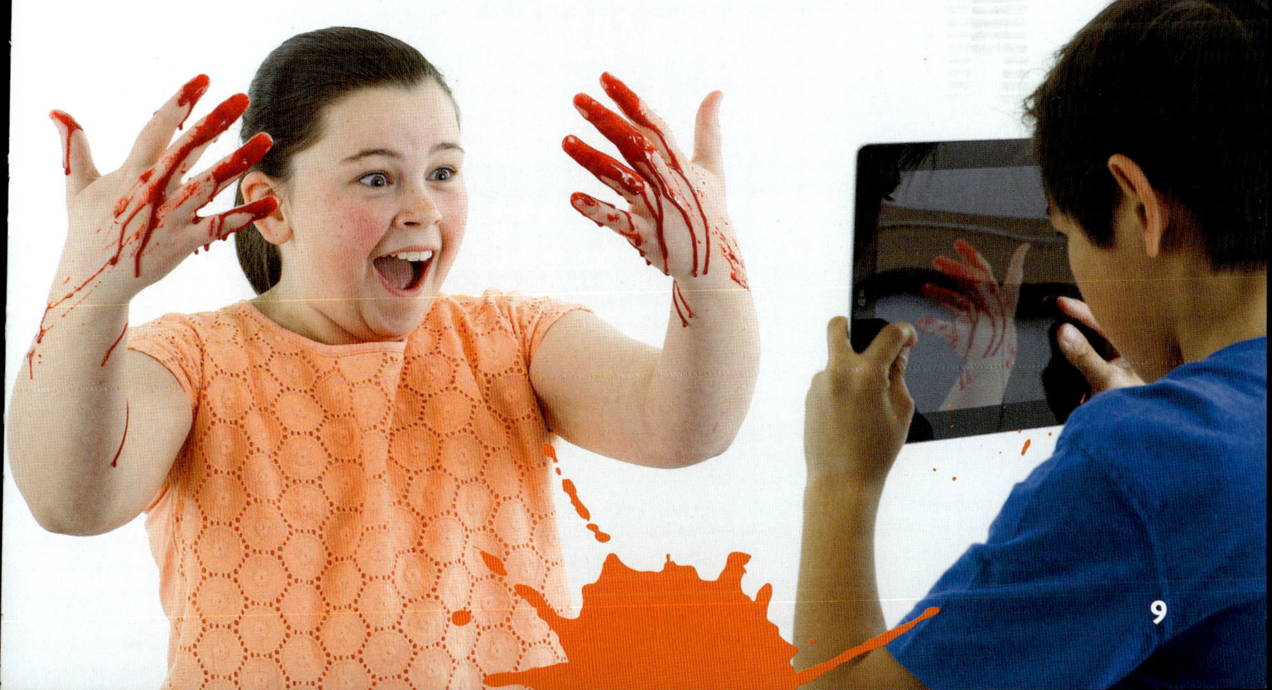

Explosions and Pyrotechnics

Few movie scenes are visually more impressive than a huge explosion. And almost nothing creates as much drama on screen. Today, on-screen explosions can be created using computer-generated imagery (CGI). However, sometimes real-life explosions are staged on a film set, particularly for action movies.

Setting up an explosion can be a dangerous process and needs to be done carefully. When a film script requires an explosion, **pyrotechnics** experts create the effects.

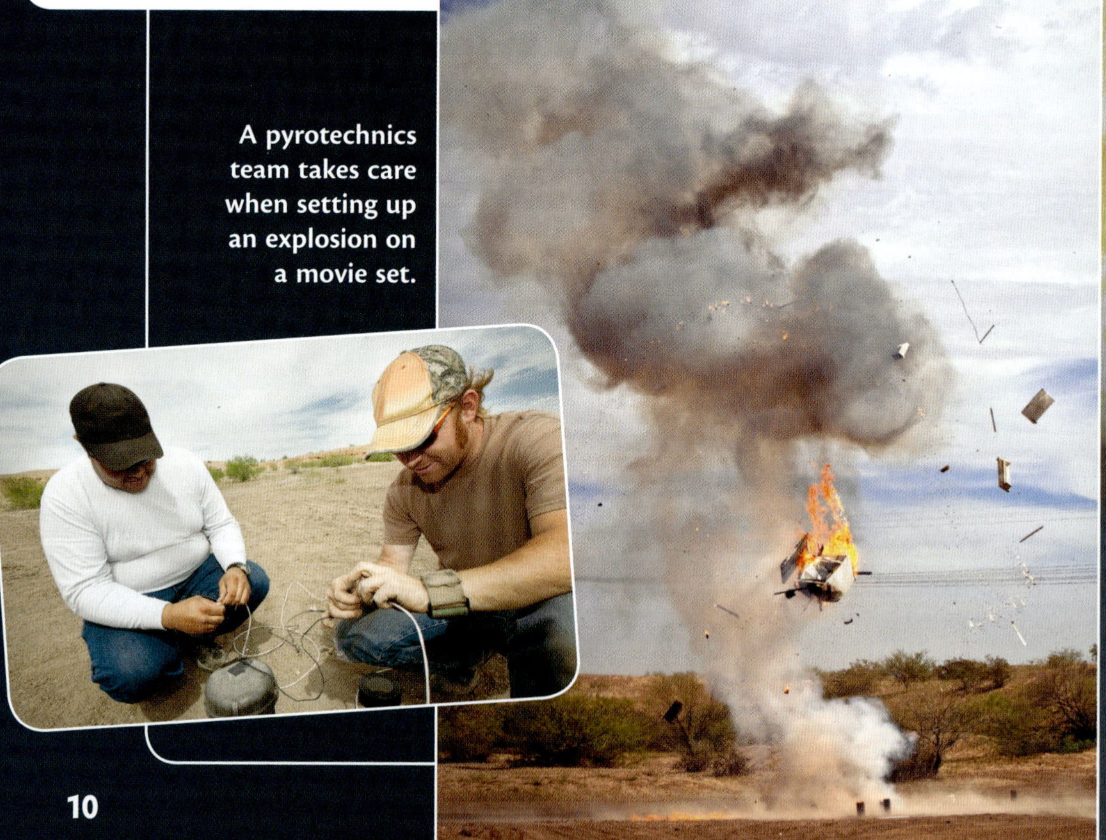

A pyrotechnics team takes care when setting up an explosion on a movie set.

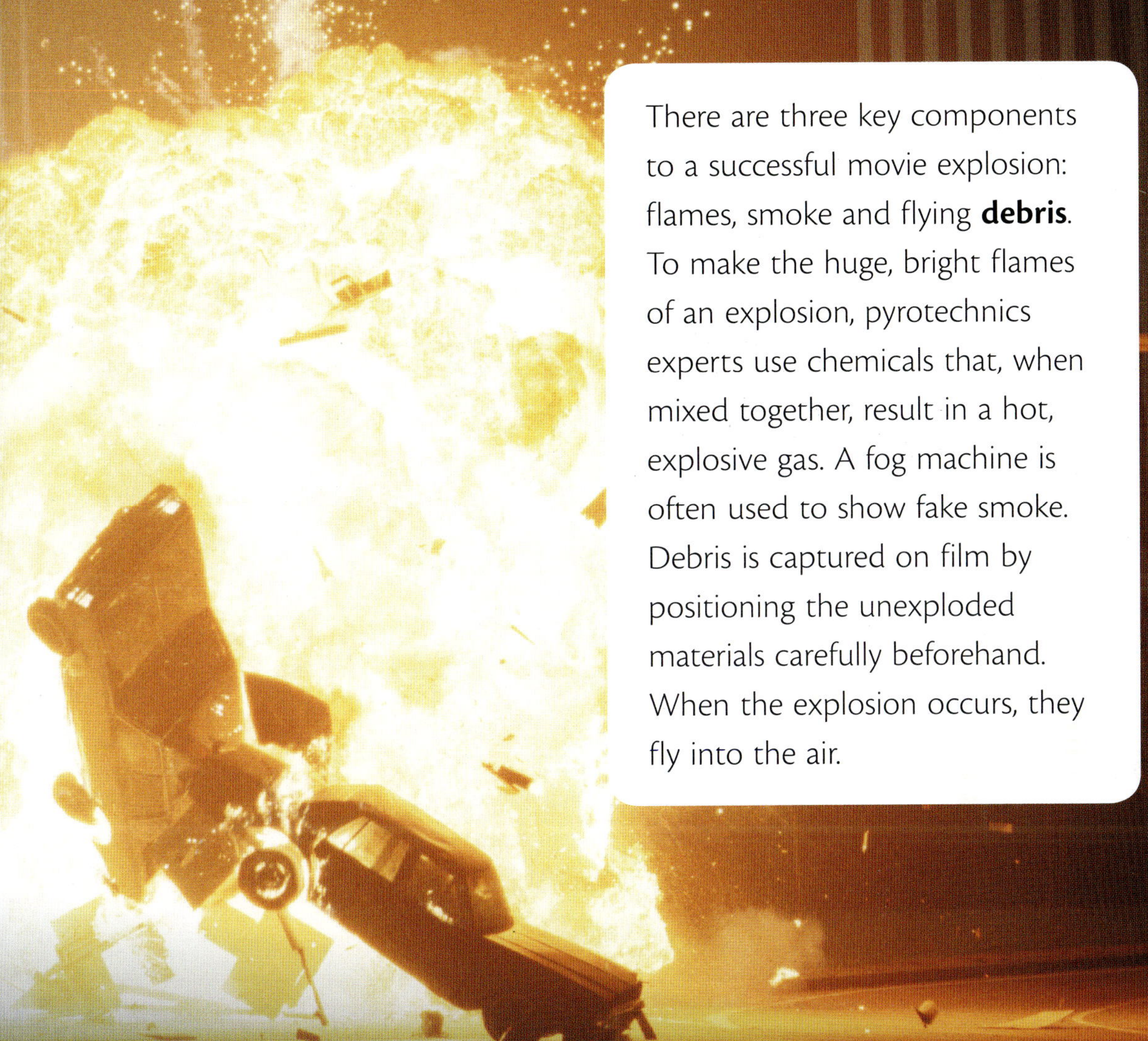

There are three key components to a successful movie explosion: flames, smoke and flying **debris**. To make the huge, bright flames of an explosion, pyrotechnics experts use chemicals that, when mixed together, result in a hot, explosive gas. A fog machine is often used to show fake smoke. Debris is captured on film by positioning the unexploded materials carefully beforehand. When the explosion occurs, they fly into the air.

Think and Talk About ...

An explosion can be done as a special effect, created on set using explosive materials, or as a visual effect, created later on a computer, using CGI technology.

Two cars explode in a scene from the movie *Dark Breed* (1996).

Motion Capture

Motion capture, or "mo-cap", is when an actor's movements or facial expressions are captured so that they can be changed into a digital form for an animated film or character.

The Rotoscope

The first attempts at motion capture on film are believed to have been made by an **animator** named Max Fleishner in 1915. He invented a device called the Rotoscope. This device traced over film footage that had been acted out by humans. It then recreated the action as animation.

Famous **film producer** and **entrepreneur** Walt Disney was impressed by the Rotoscope and how it could be used to create very realistic animations. In 1937, he used it to make his first full-length animated film, *Snow White and the Seven Dwarves*. First, actors were filmed performing the entire script. Then, animators used the Rotoscope to change the live images into animation.

The Rotoscope was used to turn the movements of actress Marge Belcher into the animated character of Snow White.

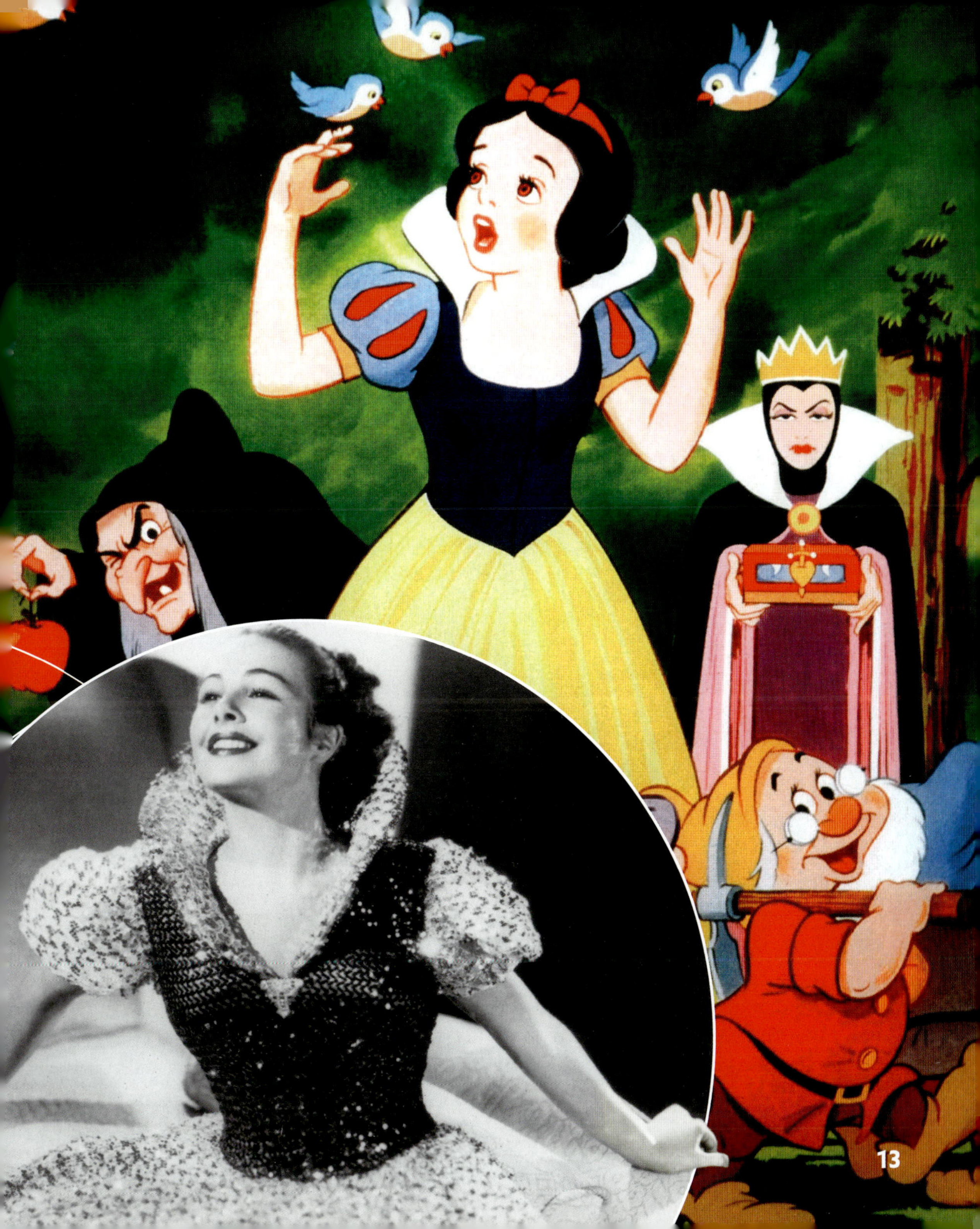

Optical Mo-Cap

The techniques used for motion capture have changed a lot throughout the decades. Tracing figures on film has now been replaced by a process called "optical mo-cap". This requires an actor to have **sensors** placed at certain points on his or her face or body before performing a scene. Signals captured by these sensors are transferred directly onto computers. The actor's exact movements can then be used to animate a digital character.

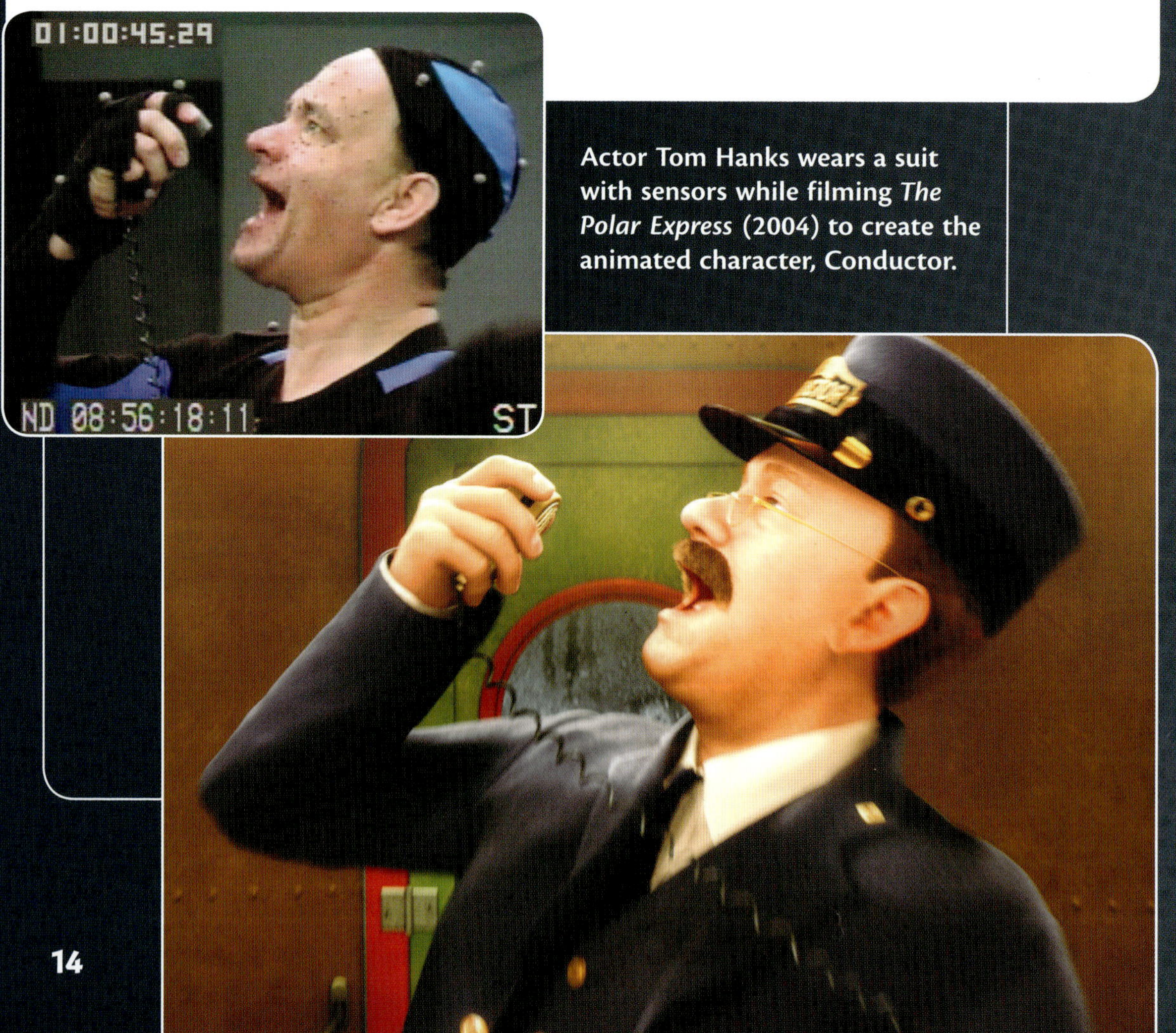

Actor Tom Hanks wears a suit with sensors while filming *The Polar Express* (2004) to create the animated character, Conductor.

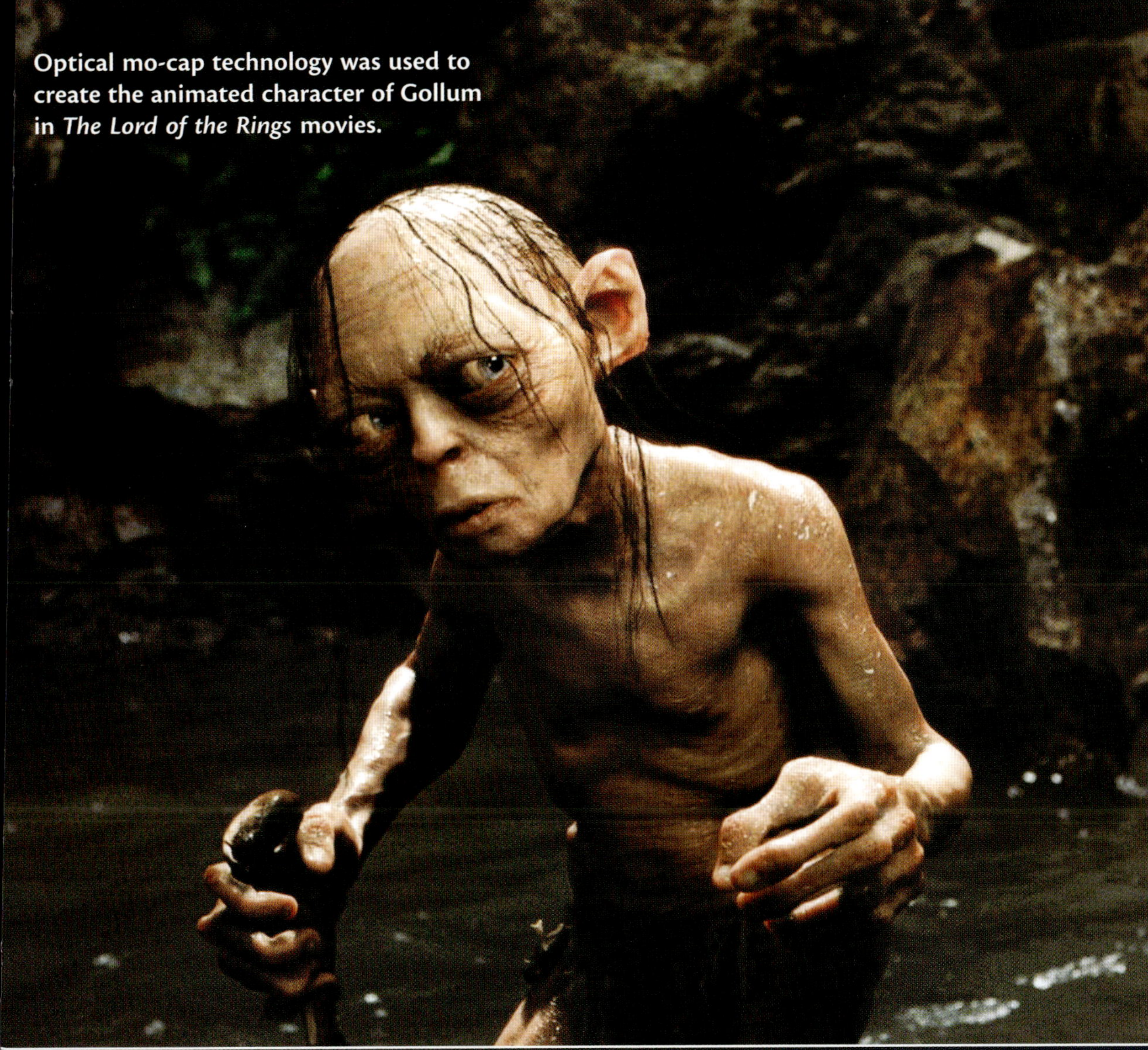

Optical mo-cap technology was used to create the animated character of Gollum in *The Lord of the Rings* movies.

Think and Talk About ...

Mo-cap has become such a common part of movie-making that some actors are chosen for roles because of their ability to work with mo-cap technology.

Miniatures

Miniatures are models that are filmed in such a way that they look like they would in real life. Most miniatures are tiny. Film-makers use miniatures when it is too expensive or difficult to film the real thing.

The first film-makers to use miniatures were thought to be Albert Smith and J. Stuart Blackton, who formed the Vitagraph Film Company in the late 1890s. They made a movie called *Battle of Santiago Bay* in 1898, based on an actual battle that took place between the naval ships of the USA and Spain in the same year. It is believed that Smith and Blackton were forced to use miniatures after they claimed to have footage of the battle. They did not have any footage, but they recreated it in a bathtub using model ships. The miniatures looked so realistic that the battle scenes in their movie were mistaken by audiences to be real.

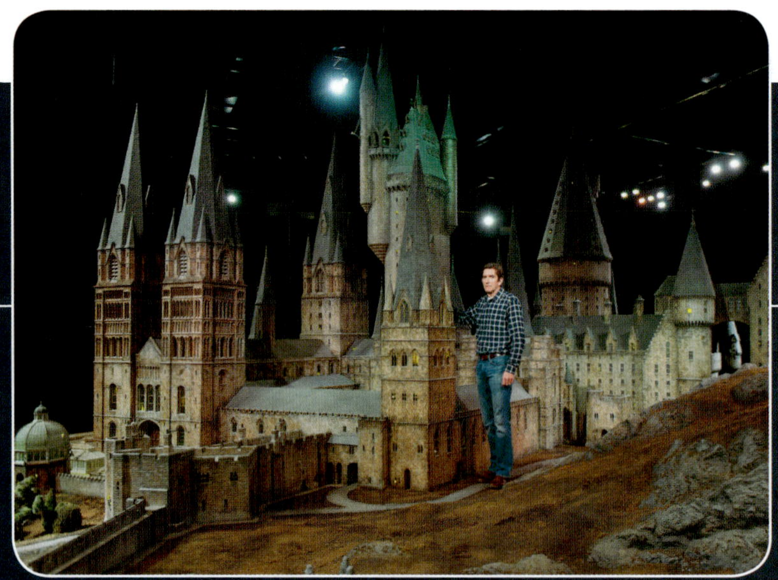

A model-maker stands in front of a model of Hogwarts Castle, built for the movie *Harry Potter and the Philosopher's Stone* (2001).

One of the most popular action movies of all time is *Indiana Jones and the Temple of Doom* (1984). In it, there is an exciting chase scene involving mine cars hurtling through tunnels. The whole scene was created using action-figure models sitting in minature mine cars about 25 centimetres long. The miniature mine cars were filmed with a small camera at a slow speed – one frame, or still photograph, at a time. When the frames were joined together, the cars appeared to be racing along the tracks at a realistic speed for normal-sized cars.

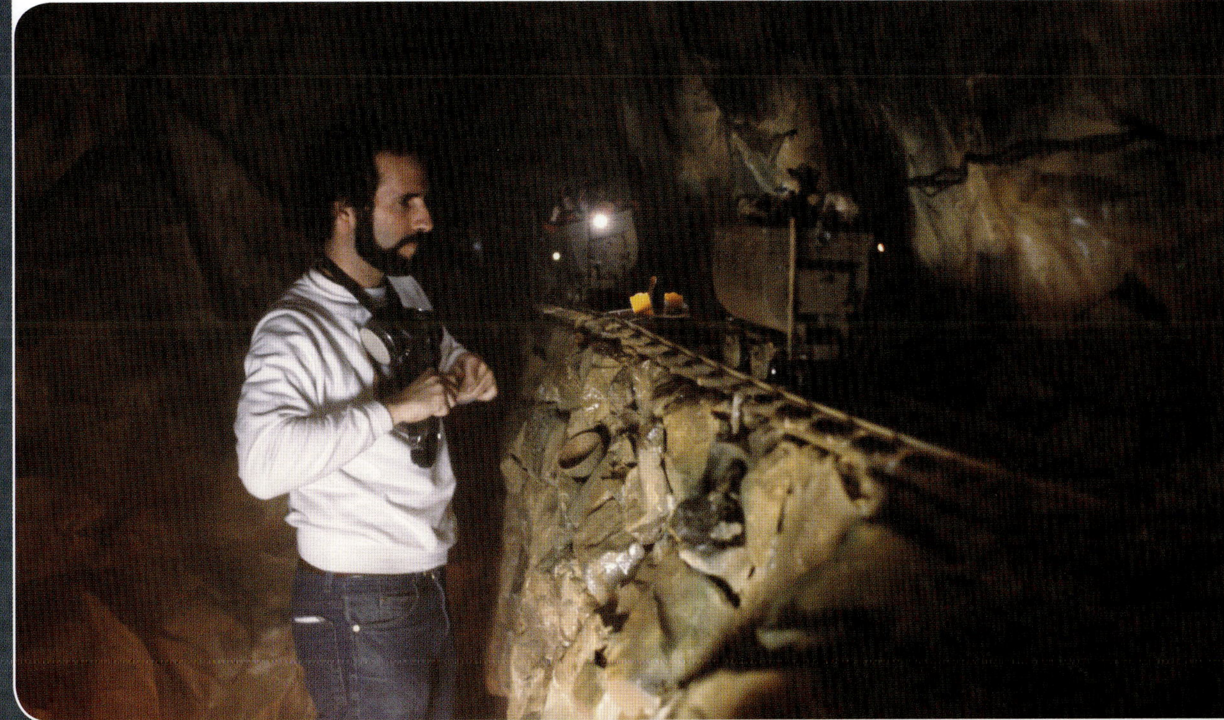

To create the mine-car chase scene in *Indiana Jones and the Temple of Doom*, film-makers built a model set with miniature figures and cars.

Animatronics

Animatronics are robotic models that appear real and move in a lifelike fashion. They are made from materials such as **silicone**, steel and electronics. Animatronics are often used in science-fiction movies, as an alternative to CGI and elaborate costumes.

Walt Disney created detailed animatronic models for his theme park, Disneyland, in the 1960s. The first animatronic model to appear on film was in the Disney movie *Mary Poppins*, in 1964. The model was a robin that whistled along with the lead actor, Julie Andrews, to the song "A spoonful of sugar".

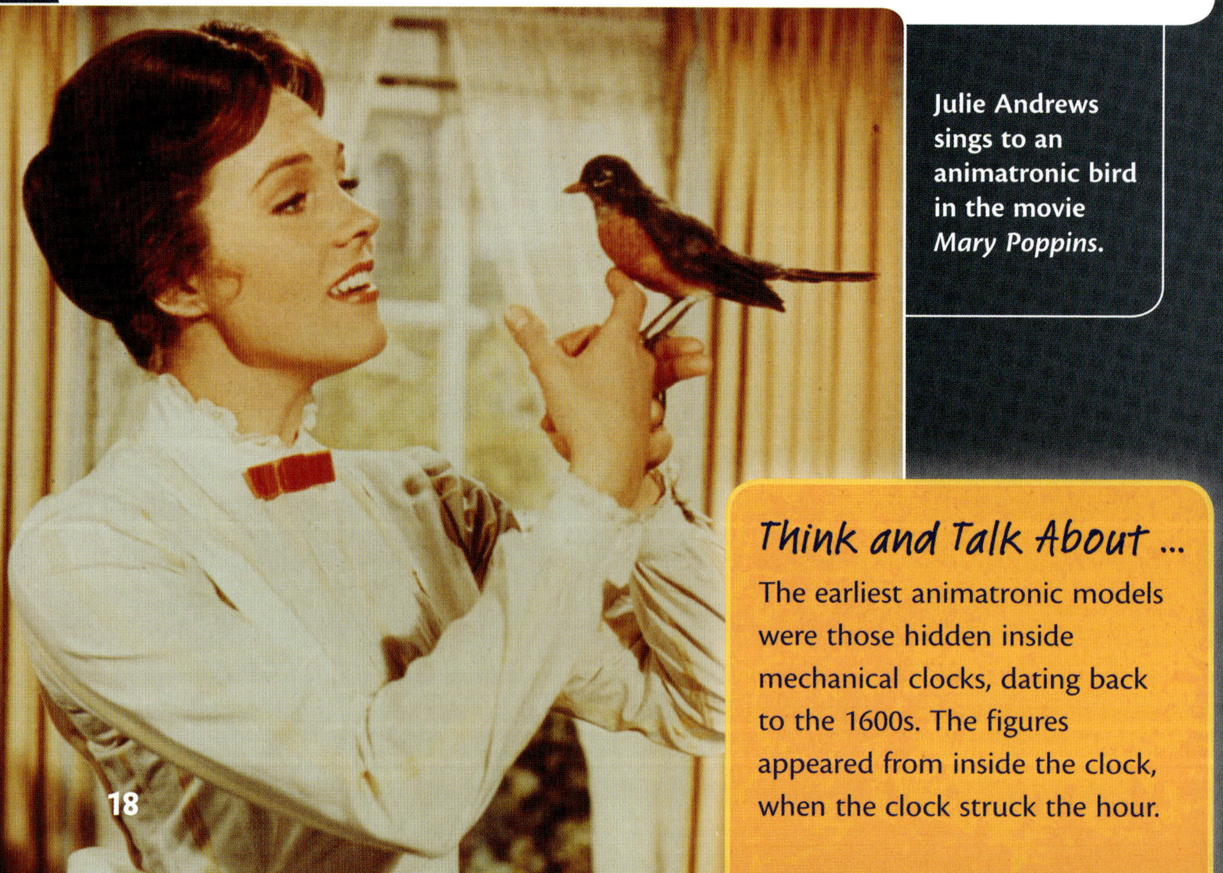

Julie Andrews sings to an animatronic bird in the movie *Mary Poppins*.

Think and Talk About ...

The earliest animatronic models were those hidden inside mechanical clocks, dating back to the 1600s. The figures appeared from inside the clock, when the clock struck the hour.

One of the most popular animatronic figures in movie history is the character E.T., from *E.T. the Extra-Terrestrial* (1982). The models built for E.T. had 150 different movements, including facial expressions, hand movements and finger gestures.

The character of E.T. has a finger that glows.

When it was made in 1993, the movie *Jurassic Park* was responsible for the largest animatronic characters ever created. Its life-sized Tyrannosaurus rex was more than 10 metres long and weighed 9 tonnes. Not all of the *Jurassic Park* animatronics were complete models – some were only the top half, while others were only the bottom half. Some of the dinosaur figures were created entirely using computers.

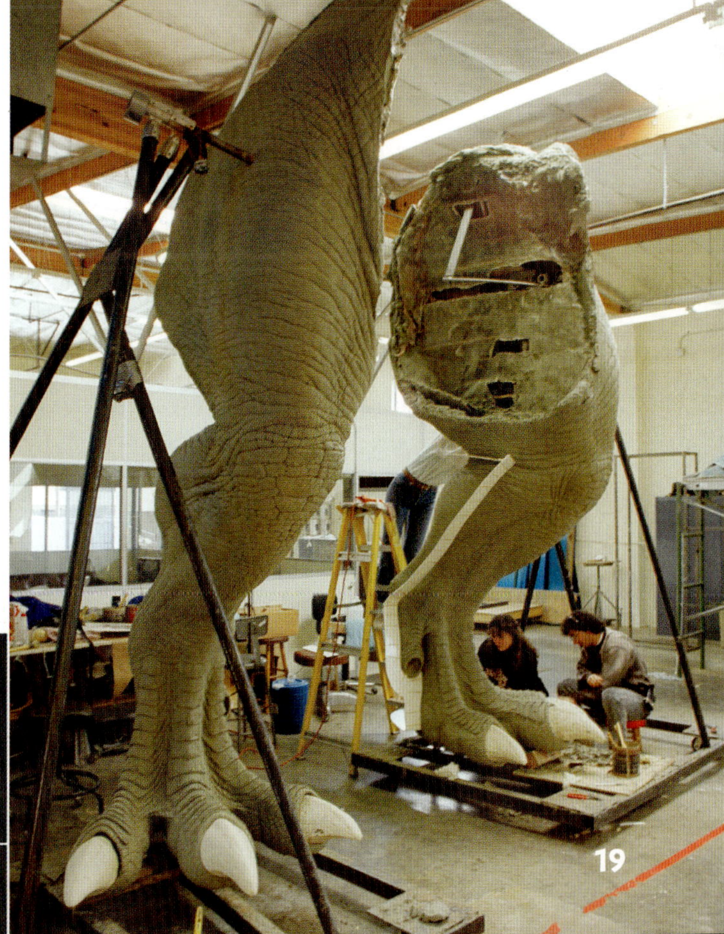

Model-makers create the first Tyrannosaurus rex animatronic model for *Jurassic Park*.

Chroma-Keying

Chroma-keying is the process of cutting out one image from a piece of film and replacing it with another image. This is done by filming a subject, such as a person, in front of a green or blue backdrop, or screen. The screen is then replaced by another image, using a computer. Green or blue screens are used because these are the colours most different from human skin tones. This makes them easier to replace digitally, when people are filmed in front of them.

An everyday example of chroma-keying is a weather report on television. The weather reporter appears to be standing in front of a map, but is actually standing in front of a blank green screen. The green screen is replaced with an image of a weather map, using a computer. The weather reporter knows where to point on the map by looking at TV screens around them. The screens show the weather map as it appears to viewers.

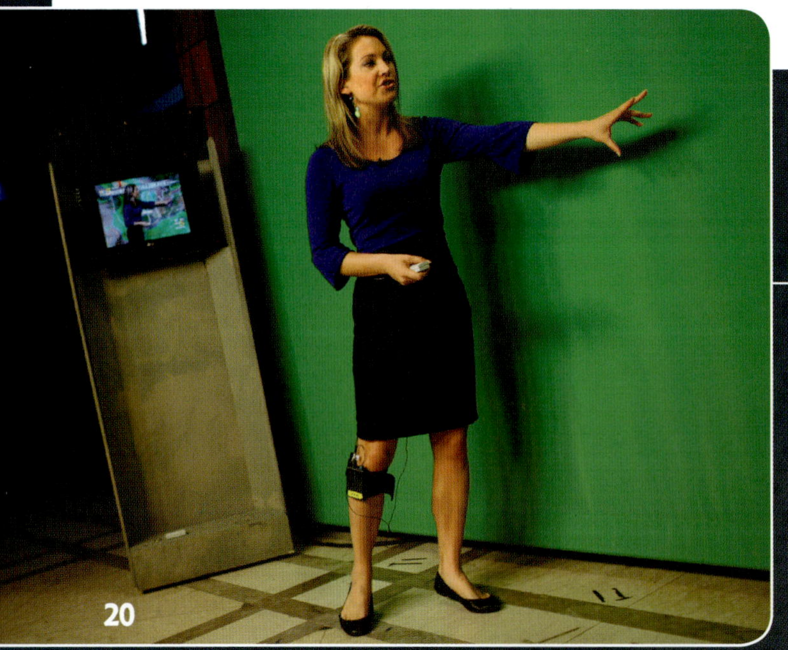

A reporter stands in front of a green screen to give a weather report.

Directors need to consider a number of things when using the chroma-keying technique.

- If a person or character is green, or dressed in green clothing, a blue screen can be used instead of green, otherwise it is too hard to separate the subject from the background on a computer. The character of Green Goblin in *Spider-Man* (2002) had to be filmed against a blue screen.
- The subject needs to be as far from the screen as possible. This avoids shadows appearing on the screen and reflections appearing on the subject.

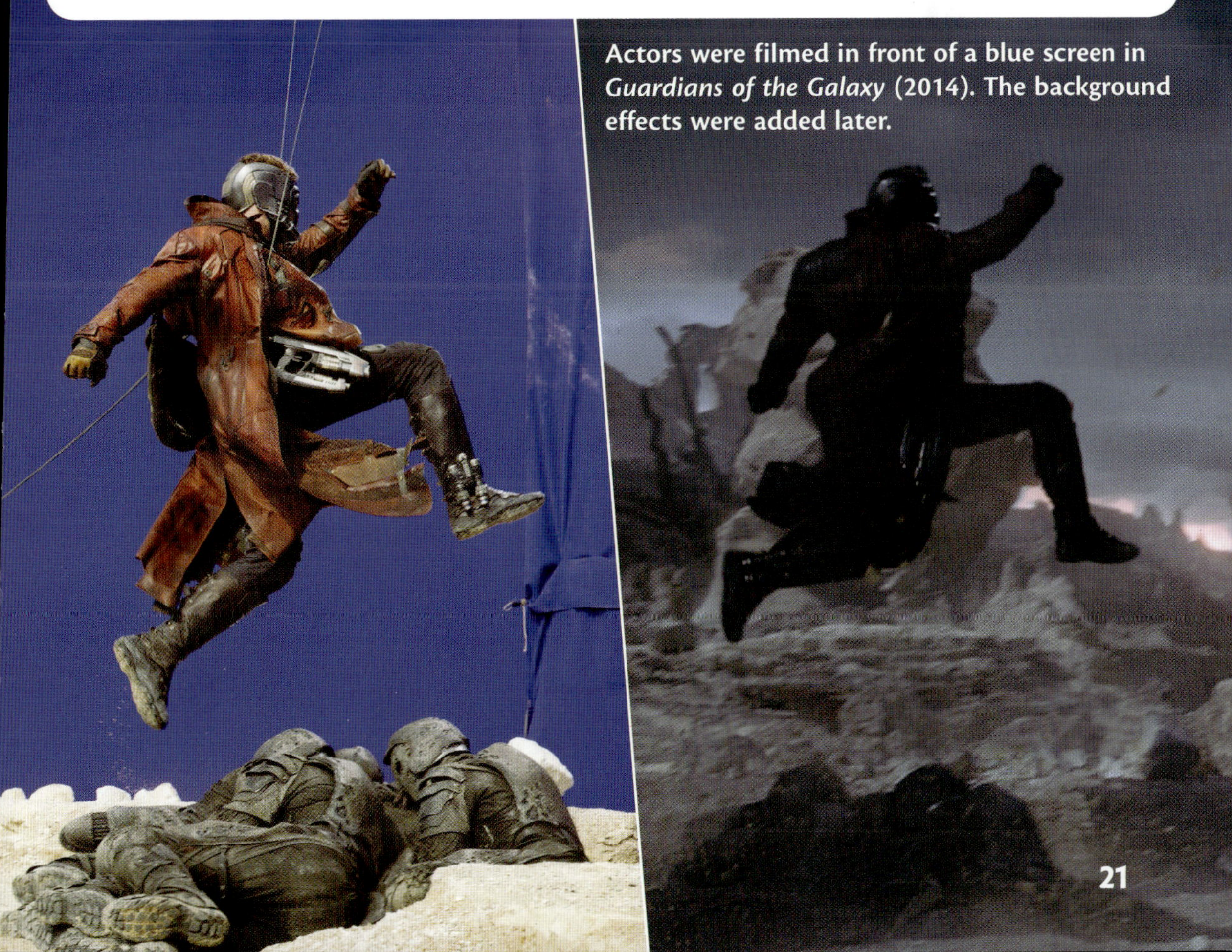

Actors were filmed in front of a blue screen in *Guardians of the Galaxy* (2014). The background effects were added later.

3D Movies

A 3D movie gives audiences the impression that the action on screen is three-dimensional, or as it appears in the real world. Film-makers began thinking about 3D technology as soon as movies were invented. The first 3D movies involved screening film footage on two separate screens. Viewers would use a device called a "stereoscope" to view the film. Each eye would take in different perspectives, which together would form a 3D effect.

Think and Talk About ...

Stereographs were small cards with two copies of the same picture printed on them, side by side. When looked at through a stereoscope, the picture appeared to be three-dimensional.

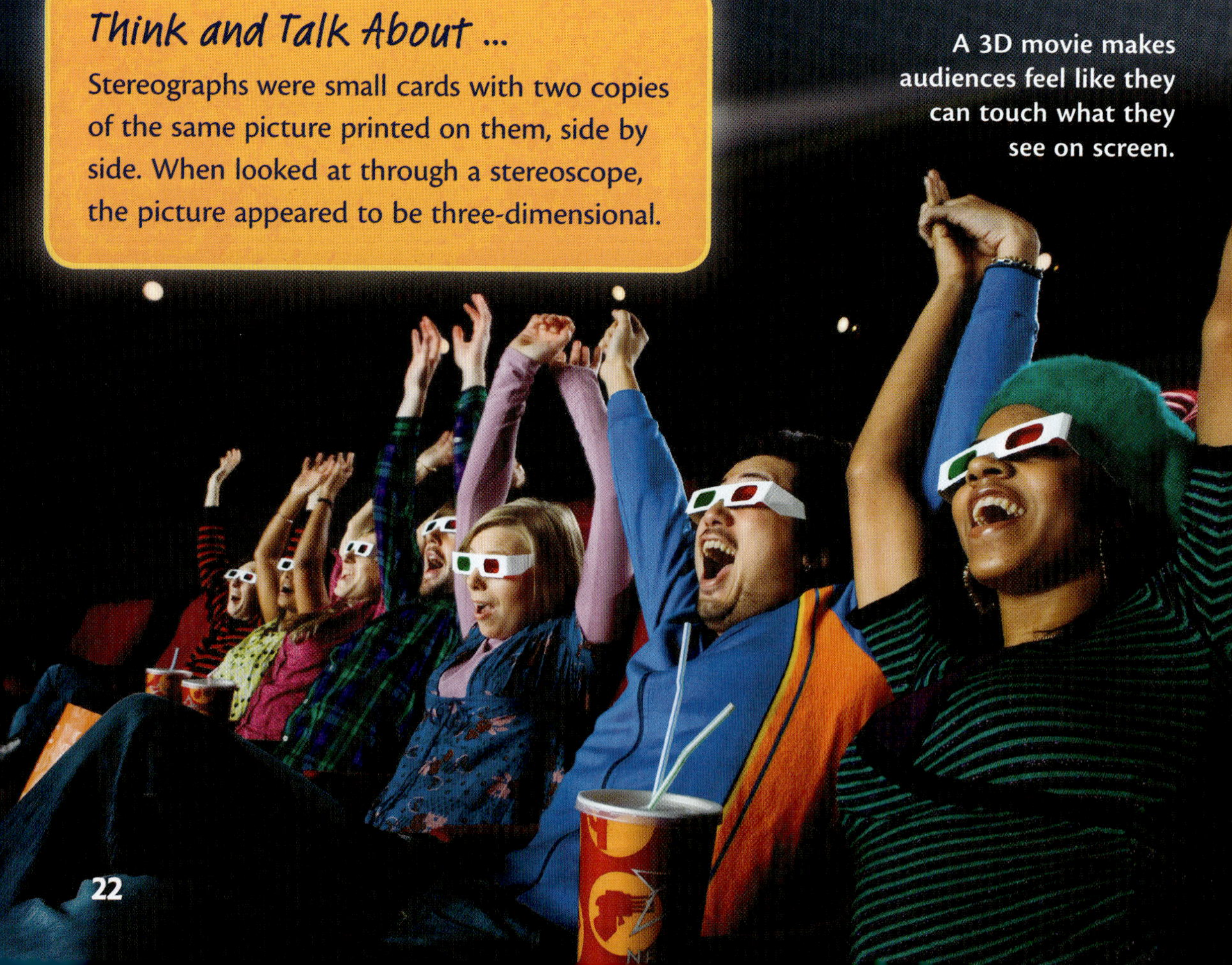

A 3D movie makes audiences feel like they can touch what they see on screen.

To make a 3D movie today, film footage is recorded by two camera lenses positioned next to each other. When the movie is shown, the two reels of film are **projected** separately: one through horizontal **filters**; the other through vertical filters. The 3D glasses worn by the viewer have similar filters, one in each lens. The human brain puts the two images together, so they appear to be three-dimensional.

How a 3D Movie Works

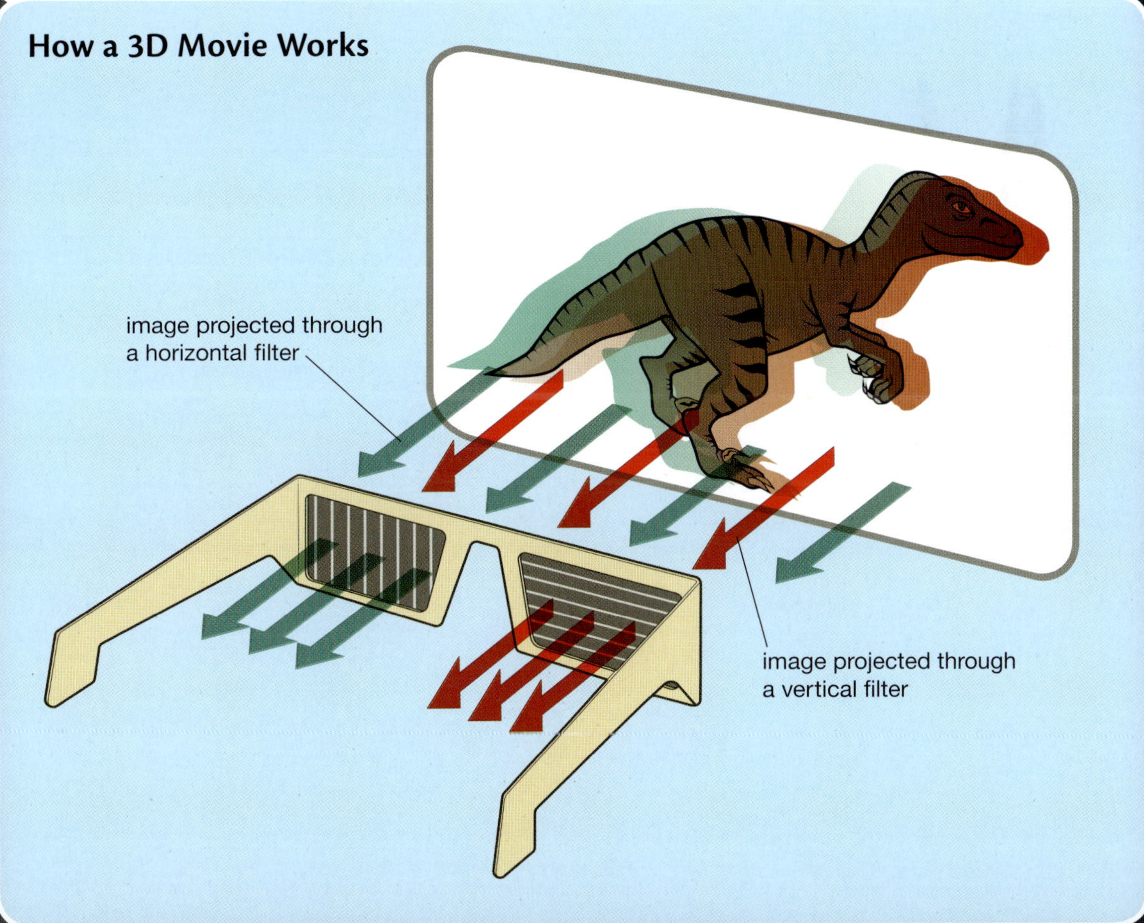

Computer-generated Imagery

Computer-generated imagery, or CGI, is a visual effect that is produced on computers. Before CGI, animation involved artists drawing and colouring in images on transparent, or see-through, sheets, known as cels. These cels were placed on top of each other to produce a single scene. Today, computers are used to produce characters, scenes, even entire worlds that are realistic or very complex.

The movie *Young Sherlock Holmes* (1985) featured the first realistic, animated CGI character. It was a character that appeared to emerge from a stained-glass window. This was considered a major advance in CGI technology.

The first animated CGI movie was *Toy Story* (1995), while the first full-length movie to feature a complete, realistic CGI world was *Avatar* (2009).

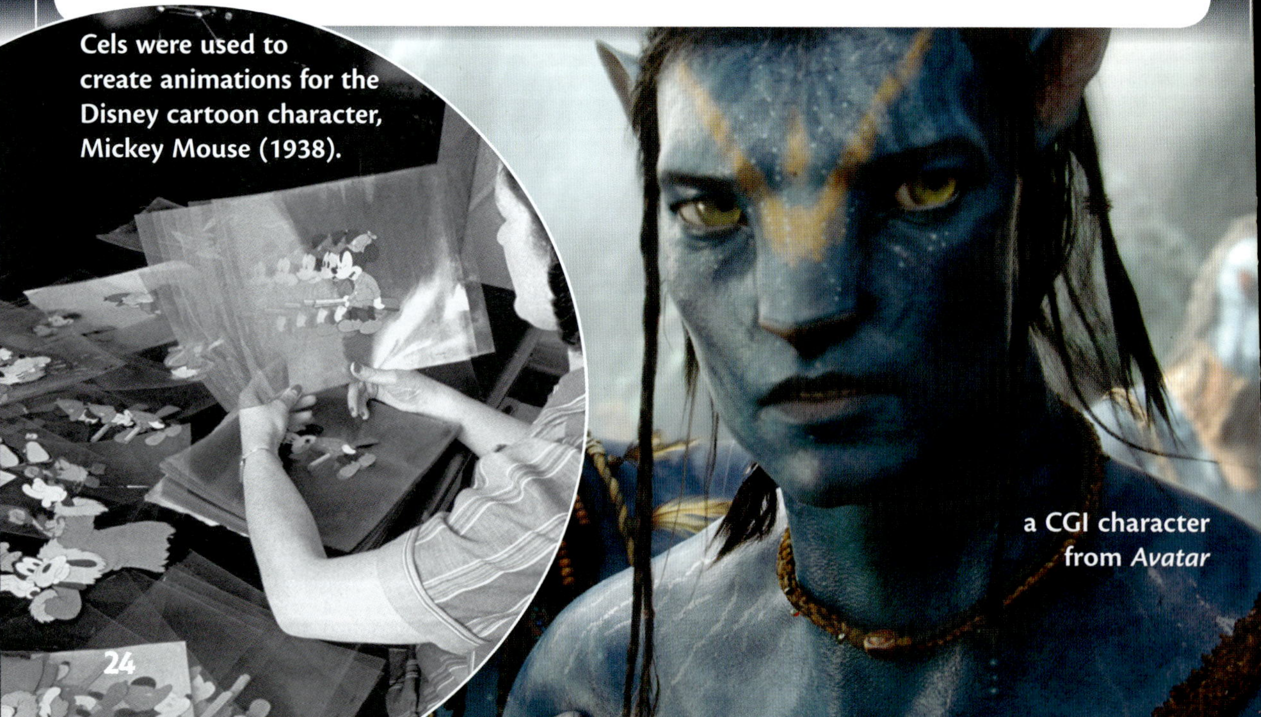

Cels were used to create animations for the Disney cartoon character, Mickey Mouse (1938).

a CGI character from *Avatar*

A Spectacular Future

Since the very beginnings of the film industry, audiences have been delighted and entertained by special effects and how they can enhance a movie. Special effects can make things on screen appear and disappear in a flash; blood, battle scenes, dinosaurs and aliens can seem real; animated characters can behave in a lifelike way; on-screen action can appear three-dimensional; or entire imaginary words can be brought to life. Only the methods used to achieve these effects have changed over time. With technology always improving, there is no limit to what visually breathtaking scenes audiences might see in the future.

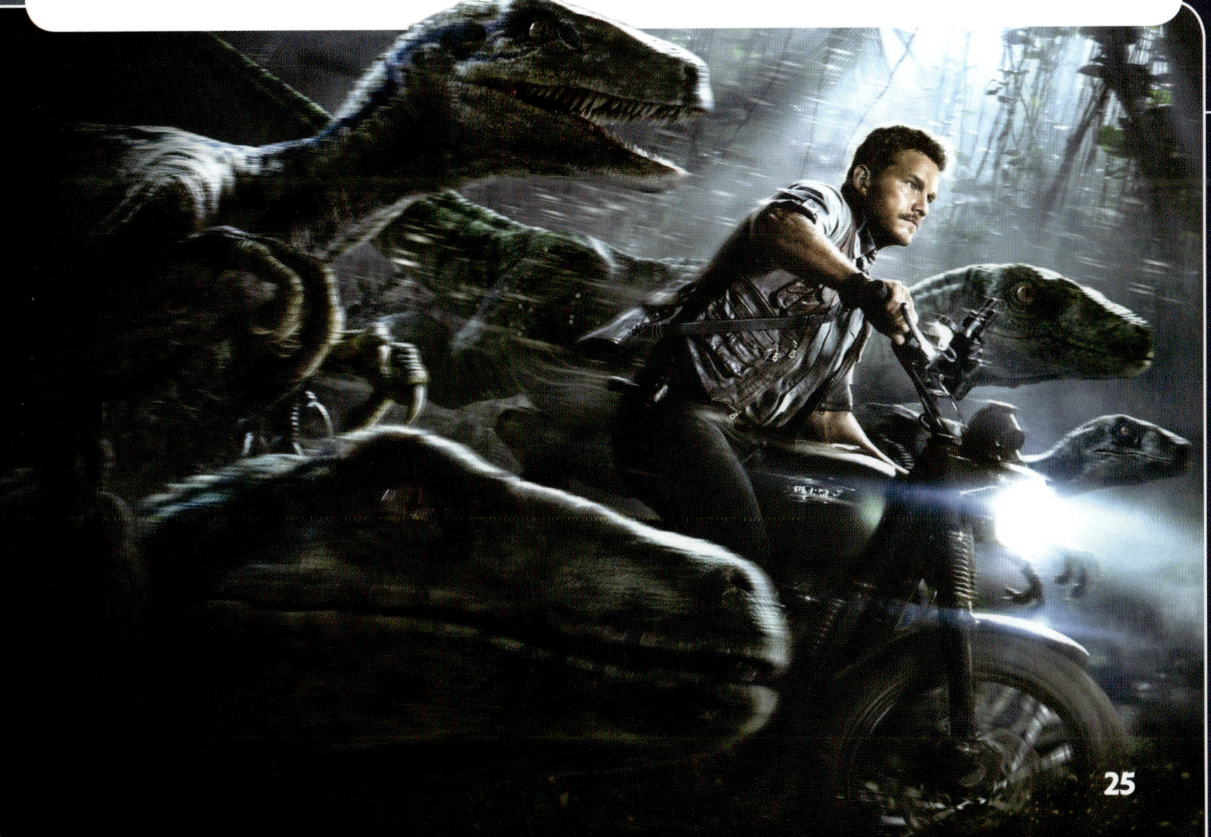

Experts in Special Effects

Some companies are formed just to provide the film industry with special effects. The people who work in this field are experts at making movies look amazing.

Industrial Light and Magic

Industrial Light and Magic is a special-effects company that was formed in 1975 by American producer and director George Lucas. It was created when Lucas was preparing to film his ground-breaking movie, *Star Wars*. He could not find a company that was able to provide him with the special effects he wanted, so he started his own, with some of the world's best experts working for him. All science-fiction movies made before *Star Wars* had been set in a universe that was empty and black. However, Lucas wanted to portray a fictional universe that people lived in, and that looked realistic. His special-effects teams created animation and computer technology, and built miniatures, models and robots, to give Lucas the effects he wanted.

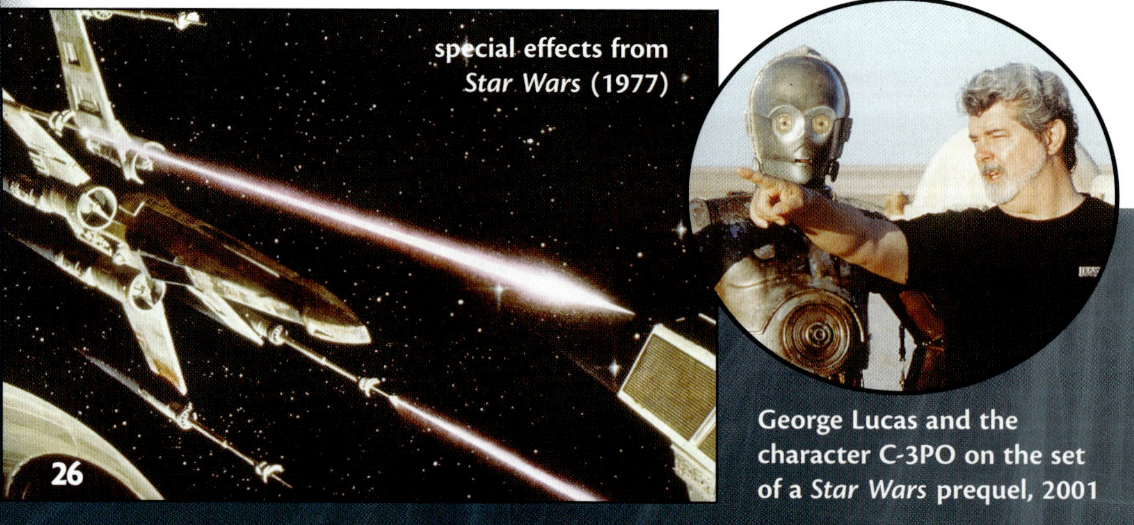

special effects from *Star Wars* (1977)

George Lucas and the character C-3PO on the set of a *Star Wars* prequel, 2001

Industrial Light and Magic has created special effects for many well-known movie series, including:

- *Star Wars*
- *Back to the Future*
- *Harry Potter*
- *Indiana Jones*
- *Jurassic Park*
- *Pirates of the Caribbean*

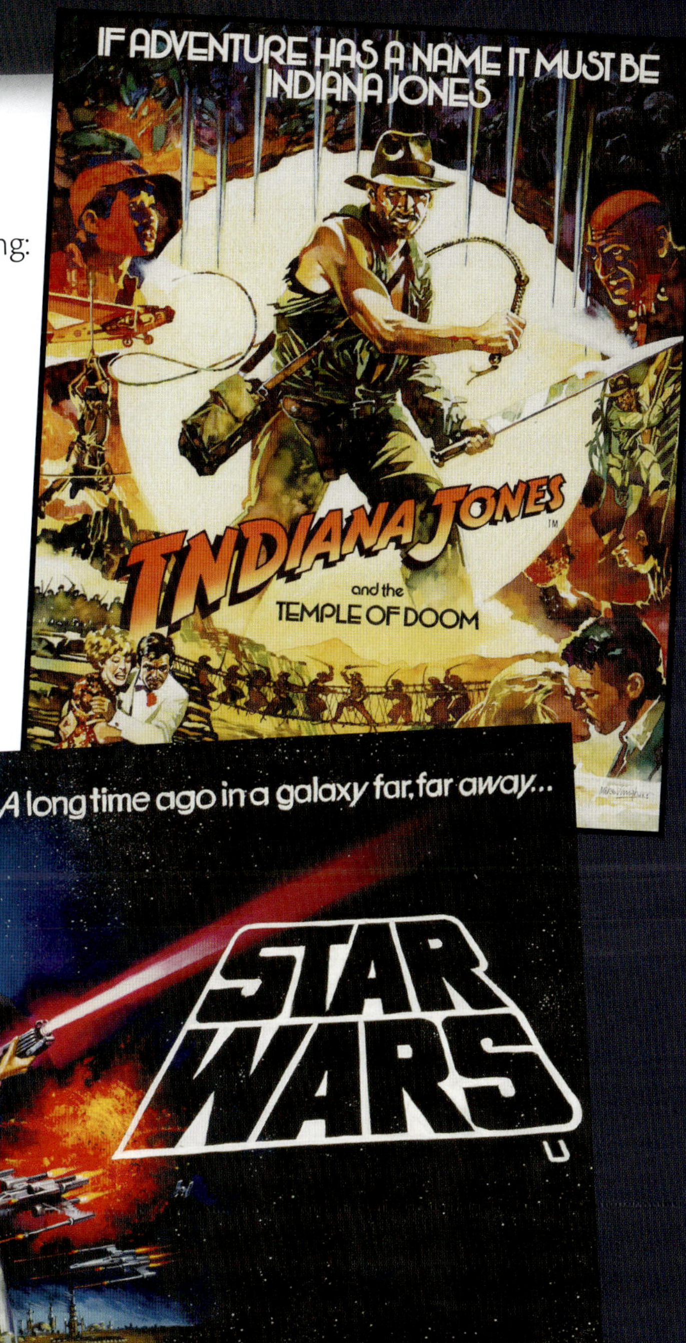

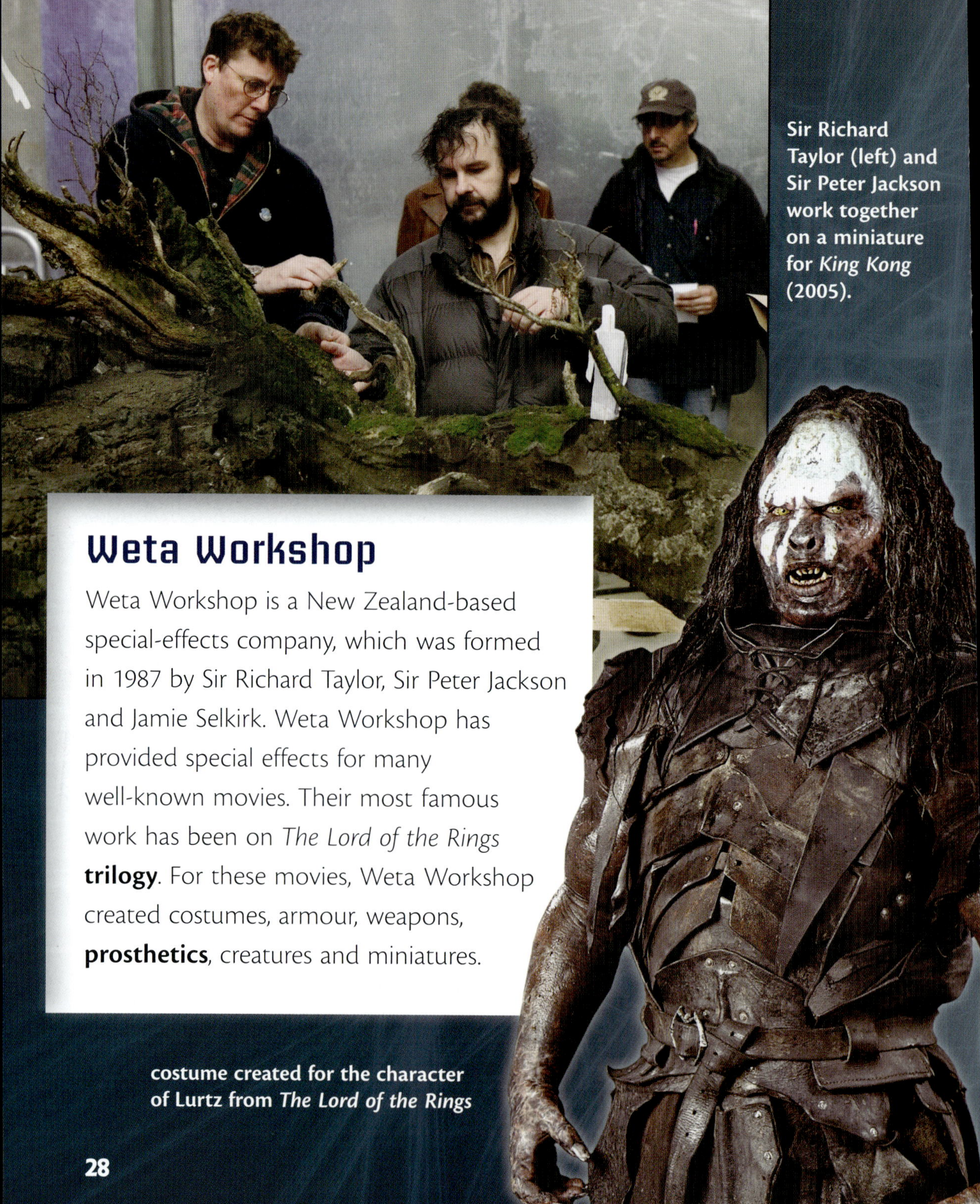

Sir Richard Taylor (left) and Sir Peter Jackson work together on a miniature for *King Kong* (2005).

Weta Workshop

Weta Workshop is a New Zealand-based special-effects company, which was formed in 1987 by Sir Richard Taylor, Sir Peter Jackson and Jamie Selkirk. Weta Workshop has provided special effects for many well-known movies. Their most famous work has been on *The Lord of the Rings* **trilogy**. For these movies, Weta Workshop created costumes, armour, weapons, **prosthetics**, creatures and miniatures.

costume created for the character of Lurtz from *The Lord of the Rings*

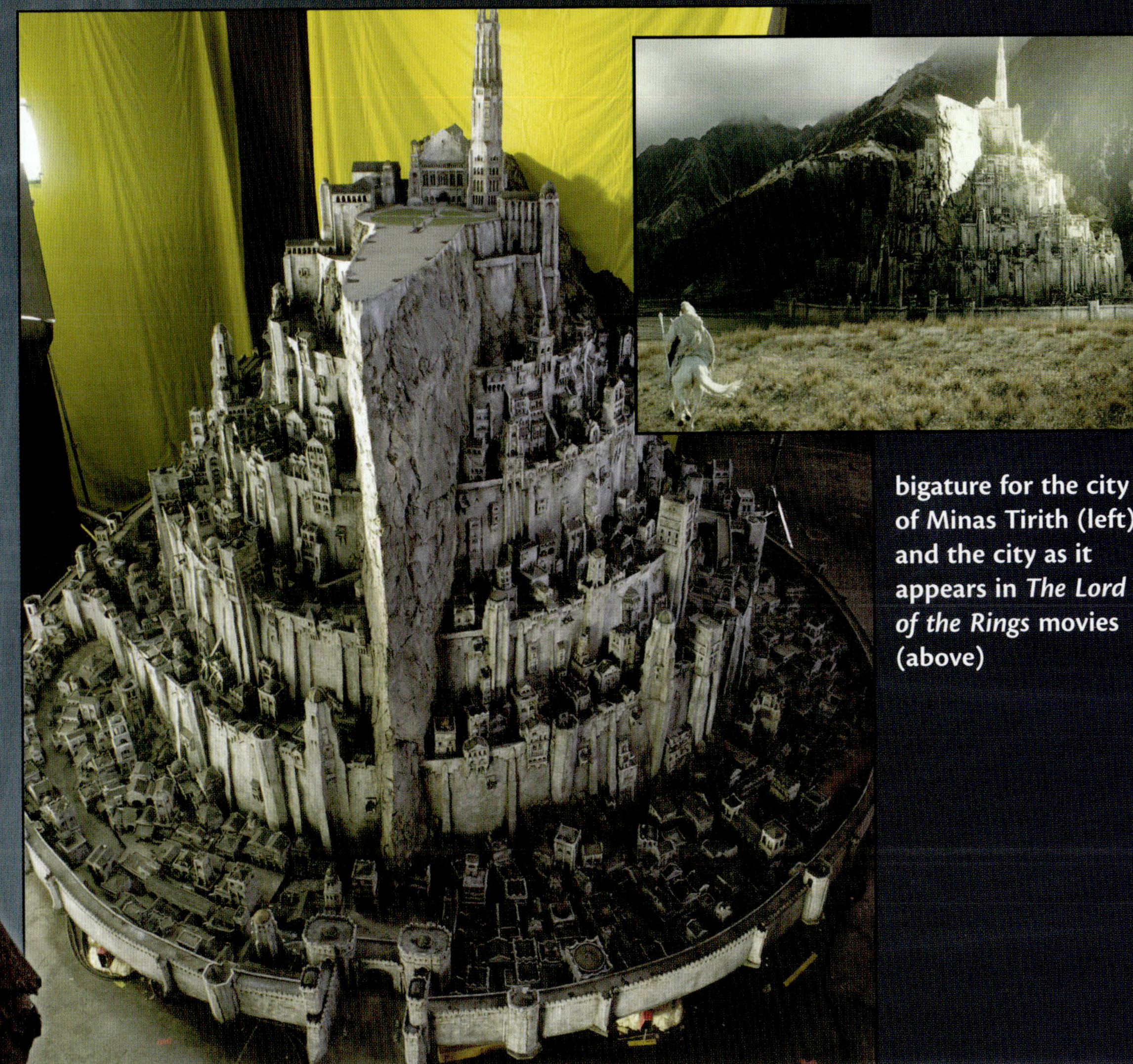

bigature for the city of Minas Tirith (left) and the city as it appears in *The Lord of the Rings* movies (above)

Bigatures

"Bigatures" is a term used by Weta Workshop to describe the models they build that are larger than miniatures, but smaller than real life. Many bigatures were created for *The Lord of the Rings* trilogy. The most detailed bigature was the fictional city of Minas Tirith, for which about 1000 houses were built.

Weta Digital

Weta Digital is a leading visual-effects company based in New Zealand. The artists at Weta Digital are famous for their innovative use of technology to create realistic characters for movies.

Creating Gollum

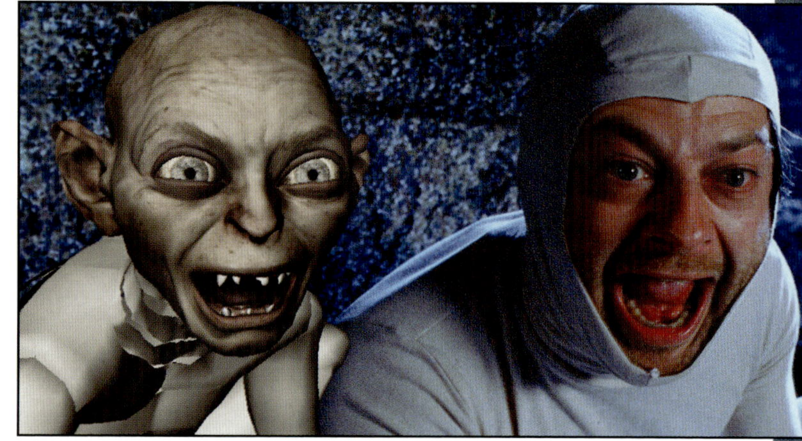

A special mo-cap suit helps capture the actions of Andy Serkis as he plays the role of Gollum.

Weta Digital created the character of Gollum in *The Lord of the Rings* trilogy. It is considered to be one of the best uses of visual effects in movie history. Gollum is a digital character whose movements appear very realistic. British actor Andy Serkis played the role of Gollum. He performed every scene in a motion-capture environment. The animators at Weta Digital then used the motion-capture data from Serkis's performance as the basis for creating Gollum – a process carried out entirely on computers.

The experts who work behind the scenes creating special effects for movies play a very important role in the film industry. Without their skill and imagination, watching a movie wouldn't be as amazing and exciting as it is for audiences today.

Glossary

animator (*noun*) — a person who creates animated movies

artificial (*adjective*) — made by humans

debris (*noun*) — the remains of something that has been broken or destroyed

director (*noun*) — a person who directs the performers in a movie or a play

entrepreneur (*noun*) — a person who starts a business and is willing to risk loss in order to make money

film producer (*noun*) — someone who manages the production of a movie

filters (*noun*) — devices that prevent some kinds of light from passing through

pioneer (*noun*) — a person who is the first to explore a new idea

projected (*verb*) — used a camera to display a copy of an image onto another surface, such as a screen

props (*noun*) — objects used in movies or plays

prosthetics (*noun*) — artificial body parts

pyrotechnics (*noun*) — the art of displaying or making explosions or fireworks

sensors (*noun*) — devices that detect, or sense, heat, light, sound and motion

silicone (*noun*) — a chemical that does not let water or heat pass through and that is used to make rubber

trilogy (*noun*) — a series of three movies, plays or novels with the same subject or characters

Index